# A Present for Mum

T0328024

Written by Claire Llewellyn

Illustrated by Javier Joaquín

**Collins**

# What's in this story?

Listen and say

chocolate shop

bookshop

flower shop

stairs

Eddie and Kate are at the shops.

4

They want to get a present for Mum.
It's her birthday.

Eddie stops at a bookshop.

Eddie says, "Mum would like a book."

Kate says, "No. A book isn't good."

Then Eddie stops at a chocolate shop.
Eddie says, "Mum loves chocolate."

Kate says, "No. Not chocolate."

Then they come to a flower shop.
Eddie says, "Mum would like a plant."

Kate says, "No. Mum likes flowers."

They go in the shop. Kate looks at the flowers. Eddie looks at the plants.

# Kate chooses some nice flowers.

15

Kate looks and looks, but she can't
see Eddie.

She sees a person with a big plant.

# Kate runs. She goes up the stairs!

# But it isn't Eddie!

Kate runs to the flower shop.
There's Eddie!

Eddie says, "Mum would like this plant."

# Picture dictionary

## Listen and repeat

book

chocolate

flowers

plant

present

# 1 Look and order the story

# 2 Listen and say

# Collins

Published by Collins
An imprint of HarperCollins*Publishers*
Westerhill Road
Bishopbriggs
Glasgow
G64 2QT

HarperCollins*Publishers*
1st Floor, Watermarque Building
Ringsend Road
Dublin 4
Ireland

William Collins' dream of knowledge for all began with the publication of his first book in 1819.

A self-educated mill worker, he not only enriched millions of lives, but also founded a flourishing publishing house. Today, staying true to this spirit, Collins books are packed with inspiration, innovation and practical expertise. They place you at the centre of a world of possibility and give you exactly what you need to explore it.

© HarperCollins*Publishers* Limited 2020

10 9 8 7 6 5 4 3 2

ISBN 978-0-00-839651-0

Collins® and COBUILD® are registered trademarks of HarperCollins*Publishers* Limited

www.collins.co.uk/elt

British Library Cataloguing in Publication Data

A catalogue record for this publication is available from the British Library.

Author: Claire Llewellyn
Illustrator: Javier Joaquín (Beehive)
Series editor: Rebecca Adlard
Commissioning editor: Zoë Clarke
Publishing manager: Lisa Todd
Product managers: Jennifer Hall and Caroline Green
In-house editor: Alma Puts Keren
Project manager: Emily Hooton
Editor: Barbara MacKay
Proofreaders: Natalie Murray and Michael Lamb
Cover designer: Kevin Robbins
Typesetter: 2Hoots Publishing Services Ltd
Audio produced by id audio, London
Reading guide author: Emma Wilkinson
Production controller: Rachel Weaver
Printed and bound by: GPS Group, Slovenia

**MIX**
Paper from
responsible sources
FSC™ C007454
www.fsc.org

This book is produced from independently certified FSC™ paper to ensure responsible forest management.

For more information visit: **www.harpercollins.co.uk/green**

Download the audio for this book and a reading guide for parents and teachers at www.collins.co.uk/839651